I0730439

ANGEL ON HIGH

A THRESHOLD SERIES PREQUEL

YAHAVIM

For those who have faced difficult endings,
May you never lose the stars in your eyes.

Angel on High

*In the far reaches of the universe,
in the nurseries of galaxies,
angels tread the vastness of space,
leaving clouds of color and
ribbons of light in their wake.
These shepherds of stars tend
tilting planets and sing with the suns
... and listen for sneezes.
Because that's how newfoundlings
give themselves away.*

PART ONE
STARDUST AND SNEEZES

With a word, a single life winked into existence, warm as the flame of a brave candle suspended among the stars. The newly-formed angel was perfect from the tips of his ears to the wiggle in his toes. His heart fluttered, and he wondered why the voice had sounded familiar. *Is this a dream?* He tipped his head to one side as thoughts became ideas, and understanding grew. *I was a thought. Was I a good one?*

"Very good."

His breath caught, for he knew Who was with him. And why. A hundred questions whirled through the angel's mind before settling into orderly patterns, neat as a row of books on a shelf. *This is my beginning.*

The word came again, warmed by a smile.

And this time he recognized it. *That is my name.*

"Our secret."

Opening his eyes, the boy blinked stardust from his lashes, looked into the face of his Maker, and sneezed.

"Do you have questions?"

The young angel whispered, "Who am I to question God?"

"*Ask*, child of light."

Love and reverence left him feeling tongue-tied, but if the God of heaven wanted his questions, he would surrender them. "Who am I?"

"Someone new."

"Am I Yours?"

"Mine, and Mine alone," the Creator replied, offering a scarred palm.

The boy solemnly replied, "Yours, and Yours alone."

And so they walked hand in hand. The Everlasting One told stories made from living words. He spoke of mysteries and promises and warned the angel of the terrible choice that could tear Creator and creation apart.

"I will be Faithful," promised the boy.

"As I am faithful."

"Indeed."

Sometimes, God's voice was like thunder, and His new servant wanted to hide his face. Sometimes it was a soft breeze, and he fell silent to catch every nuance. Either way, His words were good, and the boy found himself wishing he could capture them and keep them close. *But how?*

"Write them down."

Yes, that sounded right. "Is that what I must do?"

"Write them on a page. Bind them into a book," urged his Maker. "Fill an archive with the stories only you can tell. Your first heartbeat. Your first breath. Your first love."

The boy's dark eyes shone with adoration. "*You.*"

"I am going to Send you."

"Away?" the boy asked, surprised how much sadness that one word could hold.

"Where I am Sending you, you will neither see, nor hold. But you will hear and know that I am with you."

"I am Sent."

"When you are Sent, you must go. Where I ask you to stay, you must remain. When I call you back, you must return."

The young angel stood a little straighter. "Where will I go?"

"To the place where you will be found."

His head slowly tipped to one side. "How will I find my way?"

Giving His new servant's hand a gentle squeeze before releasing it, God answered, "Follow me."

The boy put one foot in front of the other, enjoying the steady rhythm of his steps. *Should I accompany them?* Words stirred in his mind, but before he could phrase them into a song, his Guide stopped.

"Where are we?"

"What do your eyes tell you, Observer?"

He slowly scanned their surroundings, not wanting to miss a single detail. Chipped bricks. Crumbling mortar. Rusted wire. Broken glass. Peeling paint. He was knee-deep in weeds, and they were surrounded by birds. In the narrow stretch of blue sky above the buildings that loomed on all sides, a golden star blazed, and he understood. "We stand upon the earth You created, where Time holds sway. This is day." Crouching down to peer intently at one of the milling fowl, he added, "And these are chickens."

"Wait here."

Straightening, the boy reached for his Creator's hand. *Already?*

"Fear not. This is the right time." With a kiss for his forehead, He said, "Soon, you will be found."

"Who will find me?" whispered the angel, opening his hand so God could slip from his grasp.

"I will Send Ofir, and he will call you friend."

The urban chicken yard was filled with fascinations. Pebbles in the asphalt. Scents on the breeze. Webs in the corners. With keen senses and a sense of wonder, the new angel memorized every dandelion tuft and spotted feather. However, his excitement soared to new heights when a *creak* and *slam* heralded his first glimpse of a human.

An old woman in tattered bedroom slippers shuffled along the alley. She clucked her tongue at the chickens and twiddled her fingers as she passed. He mirrored her greeting, but she didn't see the angel waving back.

Shadows inched along the ground, and he wondered what made *this* the right time. Very little was happening, and no one seemed to be searching for him. Suddenly, dogs started barking one street over. A cat with a puffed tail streaked past. And a worrying odor teased at the edges of the young angel's senses. Someone was coming, but he no longer wished to be found.

Kneeling behind the rickety hen house, he

peered up and down the alley. A crash rang out overhead, and he looked up in time to see colors explode in the patch of blue. *Angels, but not like me.* Protectors and Guardians with flashing faces and vivid wings tangled with fearsome enemies.

Scrapes and scratches echoed along the alley, and the boy shrank back, trying to make himself smaller. The chickens clustered uneasily around him. Did they think he could keep them safe? Or were they hiding him? He couldn't say for certain, but their ruffled feathers tickled his nose.

From the alley's shadows, a demon skulked into view, and the young angel's eyes widened … then began to water. He pinched his nose, but nothing could smother the sneeze that scattered stardust onto the crowding flock.

Even before he opened his eyes, a hand clamped over his mouth. "Gotcha," came a husky whisper.

He froze in fear, then lurched away, trying to wriggle free.

"Hey, hey, hey now. Take it easy, friend. You're safe!"

Friend? He stopped struggling.

His captor turned him around. "I'll make sure

of it," promised a mostly-grown angel with dark skin and a cap of black ringlets. "I'm a Protector. Do you know what that means?"

He traced the pattern on the older boy's breastplate. "Cherub."

"Through and through!"

"You found me."

"Newfoundlings are dead easy to track down. It's the sneezes." The Protector's wings drew closer, shielding them from danger in a swirl of lemon-yellow light. "Sit tight while my buddies chase off the bad guys."

He reached up to touch the other angel's shoulder. "Scar."

"Just a nick," the Protector replied. "Hardly worth mentioning."

Poking at a dimple, he said, "Smile."

"As often as possible. You should try it!"

He nodded gravely and glanced around, cataloging more details. "Spear."

"Never leave home without one. My sort need to be ready for a fight."

Relieved to have been found by someone so capable, the boy nudged closer. "You are Ofir."

The cherub's eyes widened. "Too right! And

who are you?"

"Your friend."

"Let's have a look at you." The older boy ruffled straight, black hair, tweaked a pointed ear, and then tapped his nose. "Caretakers usually do the finding and the naming. Should we wait for an expert?"

The young angel shook his head. "You will call me friend."

Ofir's brow creased in concentration, but then he brightened. "I know a name that *means* friend, and it suits you."

"Indeed?"

"We'll call you Koji."

"We?"

"Me and everyone I introduce you to," Ofir said, parting his wings to check on activity in the alley. "I'm posted with … uhh … uh-oh. Introductions will have to wait, Koji."

"Why?"

"Because chicken wire is flimsy stuff." The Protector's smile didn't quite reach his eyes. "We have company."

Fear thrilled through Koji. "I do not know what to do."

"Hey, hey, hey now," Ofir said in warmer tones. "Your job's dead easy. Just hold on tight."

"To what?"

Lifting Koji as if he were light as a speckled chicken feather, Ofir readied his spear and answered, "Me."

*On the fringes of heaven,
there are secret places.
Storehouses of rainbows. The
birthplaces of dew and dawn.
In these safe havens, there stand
towers of milk-white stone where
records are kept. From on high,
angelic archivists gaze into Creation,
watching to see what God will do.*

PART TWO
Milk and Honey

Being lifted momentarily distracted Koji. *Ofir's view is much higher than mine.* The new perspective so awed the boy that he didn't look beyond the flock of chickens clustered around the other angel's boots. Until they scattered.

Amidst panicked squawks and flying feathers, Koji glanced back, and his breath caught. Two demons had slipped past the line of cherubim. Rage burned in the eyes of a Fallen who was sawing at chicken wire with a jagged blade. His snarls were scary; his companion's hoarse laughter was worse.

"Here's how this works," Ofir said in low tones. "I'm the Protector, so I'll do the fighting. You're the Observer, so you bear witness."

Koji nodded shakily.

Flashing a confident smile, Ofir said, "Thanks to me, your first record can be an epic battle sequence! Trust me?"

"Trust you," he whispered.

"Trust the One who Sent me your way?"

"Always."

"Then watch close, Observer," Ofir urged. "And remember Whose you are."

The first demon oozed through the fresh gap in the fence, then lunged forward, blade slashing. Dodging the strike, Ofir blocked a second blow with the haft of his spear, then went on the offensive. He cracked their attacker over the head and, with one deft thrust, knocked the blade from the demon's gnarled hand.

Even when their enemies spewed terrible curses, Koji kept his promise. He didn't look away.

Slinking forward, the second demon wheezed, "We saw him first. Give us our pet, and we'll let you live."

Ofir didn't answer, nor was he distracted from their first foe, who was scrabbling for makeshift weapons. When the demon pitched a broken brick at them, wings soft as silk flashed forward to brush aside the missiles, then shoved the demon away.

Their plight didn't go unnoticed by the other warriors. A second Protector dropped into the fray with a rush of sapphire wings. Leveling his sword at the Fallen, he snapped, "Take the newbie out of here."

"Too right!" Ofir tucked Koji securely in lemon-yellow folds. "Hold tight!"

The boy clung fiercely as his new friend fought his way upward on the strength of one wing. Three stories off the ground, Ofir caught hold of a fire escape and waited for an opening. Deflecting a volley of stones, the cherub burst into the air again, quickly veering around the corner of one building and skimming up the face of its neighbor. Planting a boot on the roof's ledge, he shot into the sky, climbing away from the skirmish with powerful wingbeats.

Leveling off, Ofir asked, "Still with me?"

"Indeed," Koji replied breathlessly.

The cherub looped through a series of playful spirals. "And no wonder. You're clenched tighter than a baby barnacle."

"Letting go would be unwise. I do not have wings."

"But you should *enjoy* your first flight. This is what it's like to soar with eagles."

Stretching out his hand, Koji tried to touch a sky that seemed so close, yet remained out of reach. He searched his mind for words to describe the insistent tug of wind at his hair. And the way yellow wings looked against lofty blue.

"Hey, hey, hey, now! Are you *smiling*?"

Koji nodded happily.

Despite all the swooping and wheeling, Koji soon noticed that Ofir always returned to the same course. "Where are we going?"

"Won't know until we get there. But fear not! When we're Sent, there's always a way. And a way-maker."

Just ahead, a piece of the sky rippled and broke. Tucking his wings, Ofir shot through the widening portal and into a dazzling place. Koji squinted through his lashes at a brand new landscape. Vast meadows of golden flowers. A pristine tower. The sweet smell of pollen. And from every direction, the hum of bees.

"I'm not sure how much you already know, but most Observers live in the towers." Ofir backwinged into a smooth landing. "And the good news is, this is *my* tower!"

"You are not an Observer."

"Nope. Still a Protector, through and through." Setting Koji on his feet, Ofir explained, "But my post is your doorstep."

"This is my home?"

"Yours and mine!" the cherub confirmed. "Now let's get you over to Cherith. He'll want to count your fingers and toes."

Koji didn't mean to dawdle along the way, but bees were interesting. Crouching amidst the flowers, he watched the insects fulfill their God-given role. *I have a place. Will I also have a part?*

Ofir backtracked and ruffled Koji's hair. "Introduce yourself to the buzzers later. Right now, our Caretaker is waiting."

Not far from the tower, a crystal stream sparkled over white pebbles. Squat columns lined the water's edge, and as Ofir and Koji drew closer, the hum of bees intensified. Koji's nose twitched at the sweet scent wafting from the row. Tiptoeing closer, he pressed his hand to cool, white stone. Something inside smelled good, and he wondered what it would taste like. *Is this what it means to be hungry?*

"Honey," announced the angel who stepped out from behind the column. "It is said that the bread of angels tastes as if God first dipped it in honey."

Koji quietly compared this new person to his friend. Dark skin, but not as dark as Ofir's. Ropes of hair so long, the ends swished through the surrounding flowers. And in the brilliance of heaven's light, the Caretaker's dark braids gleamed purple. "You are Cherith."

"Yes, young one." He knelt and opened his arms. "Do you have a name as well?"

Nodding, the boy slipped into an embrace that swathed him in soft fabric. *Cherith's sleeves are full. Ofir's tunic has no sleeves at all. Cherith's ears are pointed. Ofir's are not.* Reaching up to check, the boy made a new discovery about himself. "My ears are like yours."

"Yes. There are similarities between our orders."

"He's Koji," Ofir offered. "Seems to be easily distracted by this and that."

"So I see." In soothing tones, the Caretaker murmured, "Fear not, Koji."

"I am not afraid."

"You are trembling."

Koji rested his cheek against Cherith's shoulder, eyes crossing as he tried to memorize the intricate pattern of stitches decorating his collar. *Cherith's embroidery is black—Caretaker. Ofir's is greenish—Protector. What color will designate an Observer like me?*

"Is this normal?" Ofir asked worriedly.

"He's a little dim, but mostly fraught." Cherith gently stroked the boy's chin-length hair. "Did you sing with him?"

"No time," Ofir admitted. "We ran into a mess of bother. Had to wing it fast."

"That explains a lot." Cherith tucked a finger under Koji's chin, lifting his face. "How many words have you gathered up, young one?"

"So, *so* many," Koji solemnly replied. "About stars … and flowers … and flowers that look like stars. And pebbles … and bricks … and birds … and blue. And clouds … and hives … and honey … and *Him*."

"Don't leave out my part," Ofir interjected. "That was some fancy flying!"

Koji nodded gravely. "I will never forget."

"You are the eyes and ears of heaven," Cherith explained. "Words are your service. Art is your joy. In due course, you will learn how to set your thoughts upon a page, but a song will do for now. Sing a song of beginnings. Tell me about your first day."

Finally! Koji's song came in a rush as he shared all of his pent up discoveries. In return, Cherith sang about the storehouse of beauty in which they stood, introducing himself as a keeper of bees and a maker of ways. Ofir even added a verse, thanking God for sneezes, spears, and safe havens.

Koji's eyes slid shut as he concentrated on the cherub's voice, which was rich with love and bright like his smile. A good voice. The voice of his friend.

But suddenly, Ofir's song took on a commanding note. An invitation. One that was soon answered by exclamations of surprise and jumbled questions. At least a dozen people filed out of the white tower and hurried forward. All barefoot. All pointy-eared. All staring.

"They are like me," Koji whispered.

"Yes." Cherith pulled the boy more securely into his arms. "But it is to *me* that Ofir was Sent. Do not let their hopes distract you."

Although Koji wasn't sure why the angel's words felt like a warning, he promised, "I will remember."

*In their youth, heaven's archivists
practice endlessly, capturing
moments with words and binding
them in illuminated books. After
many watches and seasons,
the adept reach the limit of what
their mentors can teach.
These "middlings" must wait to
see which God will Send—
another mentor to guide them, or
an apprentice of their own.*

PART THREE
SILVER AND GOLD

"He is so new!" exclaimed one of the angels from the tower.

Another said, "Hello, bright eyes."

"Is he here for one of us?"

Koji turned in Cherith's embrace for a better look at the crowd he'd drawn. The gathered Observers were like Ofir—older boys, mostly grown. And they all talked at once.

"When did he arrive?"

"How did he get here?"

Ofir spoke up. "I found him. I brought him."

"Can we keep him?" asked an Observer with tiny braids in a soft shade of jade.

"Why else would he be Sent?" his neighbor reasoned.

Koji didn't know how to answer, so he leaned back against Cherith.

"Children, you know better than to try to take what must be given." The Caretaker met each gaze. "By all means, tell me if this young one's name is under your hand or over your heart."

Feet shuffled. Shoulders drooped. Smiles turned sheepish.

"He *will* need a mentor," insisted one.

"So might you," Cherith countered. "Who can say what God has in store for those who await His call?"

"Who can say?" agreed several.

More added, "Amen and amen."

"Well said." The Caretaker rested his cheek against Koji's hair. "Can you confirm it, young one? Were you Sent to any of these?"

Focusing on the angel who'd asked to keep him, Koji gave a tiny shake of his head.

Although disappointment flickered across his face, the other Observer smiled. "Not to worry, bright eyes. You are welcome all the same."

"Thank you." Glancing up at Ofir, he added,

"I am called Koji, and Ofir is my friend."

"Too right," agreed the cherub.

"And Koji is in need of a Weaver's services." Raising his voice, Cherith called, "Is there a Weaver hereabouts?"

"Near and dear!" came the cheerful reply. "What has everyone buzzing like so many bees?"

The crowd parted, and Koji stared at the newcomer. Like the others, this angel's feet were bare, and his ears were pointed. But he wore an intricately woven turban—hair and cloth, ribbons and bells. Even after staring for several moments, Koji wasn't sure if the Weaver's hair was black or blue. *Maybe hair can come in two colors.*

"A newfoundling!" Squatting down, the Weaver offered a brown hand and a bright smile. "We don't see many of you in the fringes."

With a measure of amazement, Koji reached back and touched each of the angel's fingers, softly counting, "One, two, three, four, five … six?"

"Such is the lot of a Weaver!" Clasping Koji's hand in his, he rubbed the boy's knuckles with both thumbs.

Second thumbs, peacock stitching—Weaver. With a small start, Koji checked the collars and cuffs of the other members of his order. "Silver and gold?"

"A sure indicator of heaven's archivists," the Weaver said with a wink. "Shall I embellish your tunic in gold and silver?"

Koji glanced down at his plain raiment, then checked Cherith's face. When the Caretaker inclined his head, the boy eagerly asked, "Can I watch?"

This time, the Weaver looked to Cherith, who answered the unspoken question. "Yes. You and Ofir will tend to Koji's immediate needs. In the meantime, these good Observers and I will work out a rotation for their new pupil."

"All of us?" asked the angel with jade braids.

"Yes, Darda. *All* of you." The Caretaker released the boy. "Koji is a child in need of guidance, and you are middlings in need of confidence. Give him the benefit of your knowledge. Teach him the skills he needs to excel. Learn what an apprentice might require from you."

As a murmur of excitement spread through

the group, Ofir and the Weaver led Koji in the direction of the tower. The boy ventured, "I am a gift?"

"One we accept with all gratitude!" the Weaver replied.

Koji looked back, then forward, then up into the faces of his escorts. "My name was a gift from Ofir. My silver and gold will be a gift from …?"

"Weft," the turbaned angel supplied, giving Koji's hand a friendly squeeze. "Everyone calls me Weft."

Once he was through the tower doors, Koji stopped to stare. Balconies ringed a circular chamber, connected by winding staircases. White stone reflected cascading light, scattering fragments of rainbows. And everywhere, books.

The contents of this archive weren't confined to shelves. Piles on tables. Rows on ledges. Stacks on stairs. Koji tiptoed closer to a book standing open on a pedestal, but Ofir caught him by the back of his tunic.

"Hey, hey, hey now," the cherub said with a smile. "Before you stick your nose in a book, there are things you need up top."

Weft started up the stairs. "This way!"

Koji followed more slowly, for with every winding turn, something interesting came into view. Jars that bristled with brushes. Crumbling piles of pigment. Pans of vivid paints. Reams of gleaming parchment. And alcoves partially hidden from view by exquisite tapestries and swaths of sheer cloth embroidered with varicolored threads.

Midway through the climb, he and Ofir caught up to Weft. The Weaver peered over the shoulder of an Observer whose pen scratched lightly over the page of an open book.

"Diligent as ever, Prosper!" Ofir greeted.

"As ever," echoed the angel, whose black hair made a striking contrast to pale skin. Laying aside his pen, he laced his fingers together. "Welcome, Koji."

Weft explained, "Prosper has already begun an entry about you for the archive."

"Me?"

"Thee!" With a soft laugh, the older boy

turned his book so Koji could see. Beautiful penmanship flowed across the page, accompanied by the sketch of a solemn-faced boy reaching for a honey bee.

Koji asked, "Is that what I look like?"

"Only for a moment. Already you have changed," Prosper replied, his blue eyes alight.

"I did?" At the older Observer's nod, Koji asked, "How?"

Leaning closer, Prosper whispered, "By meeting me."

Will I change each time I meet a person? If so, I will be a different person many times. Intrigued by the prospect, Koji whispered, "Indeed."

Weft interrupted by steering the boy back toward the stairs. "Let's leave such mysteries for later discussion. Our newfoundling needs tending."

"Sending, tending, wending," murmured Prosper, who waved them off and picked up his pen.

Koji could tell that the topmost floor of the tower wasn't for Observers because the space held no books. Instead, there were looms of different types and sizes, spools and skeins of vivid thread, and enormous pots in which trees and climbing vines grew. His nose twitched at all the new smells—sweet flowers, spicy bark, sharp dyes. The various hoops suspended here and there in the greenery further piqued his curiosity.

Stepping closer to a circlet spinning on its fine strand, he stopped short at a change in texture. The rug underfoot had a floral pattern in a pleasing blend of greens and yellows. *Like the meadow.* Koji wiggled his toes, then looked back into the branches of a potted candle-tree. Spots swam before his eyes. Bright. Erratic. Confusing.

Not bees. Nor birds.

"You must be hungry," Ofir said, holding out a hand to attract one of the fluttering creatures.

"God's little providers are drawn to your need," Weft explained.

Realization dawned, bringing wonder. *Angels! These also belong to God.* The boy mimicked Ofir and held out his hand. A small person with faceted eyes and delicate wings darted closer and turned a somersault. When a translucent flake drifted onto his outstretched palm, Koji breathed, "Manna."

"The bread of angels," Ofir confirmed. "These little guys keep us from fading."

"Eat, Koji," urged Weft, who was already threading needles with gold and silver filaments. "Let my flock refresh you."

Koji murmured thanks to the manna-maker with a fuzz of magenta hair. Then he dropped the wafer of food onto his tongue. Sweetness spread pleasantly in his mouth.

"Hey, now!" Ofir grinned broadly. "Another smile. I like this trend."

From the direction of the stairs, someone called, "Beg your pardon, Weft."

The Weaver turned. "Did you need something, Darda?"

"Cherith made his decision." The Observer with jade braids held out both hands. "Are you ready, bright eyes? Your first lesson will be with me."

A child of light walks in the light.
Light sings through his veins.
Light buoys his flight.
Light touches his lips with sweetness.
Light clothes him in radiance.

PART FOUR
Look and Listen

W eft sat amidst an assortment of floor cushions, embellishing the collar of Koji's tunic. The young angel looked on as needles flashed. Although he couldn't make sense of the emerging pattern, he felt sure it held meaning. Koji checked the decorative bands edging the Weaver's collar. *There are likenesses.* A quick peek at Darda's raiment revealed more similarities, but several differences. *The intricacies are unique. And beautiful.*

"Show me your skills, bright eyes," interrupted Darda, holding an open book for Koji to see. "Can you tell me what this says?"

The boy scanned the text. "Indeed."

"Don't hold back," chided Ofir. "Strut your stuff!"

Choosing a portion, Koji's fingertips skimmed over living words. "God, the blessed and only Ruler, the King of kings and Lord of lords, Who alone is immortal and Who lives in unapproachable light."

Darda said, "Approved! You have all your wits. But reading is the easy part. The rest takes a lifetime to learn."

My life is an eternity. Will I never stop learning? Koji asked, "Will you teach me to read my raiment?"

Trading a look with Weft, Darda admitted, "I cannot teach you Weaver's patterns. Observers only write in heaven's language."

Koji accepted this with a nod, but his gaze rested longingly on Weft's cuff. *There is a message there, hidden in plain sight.*

The Weaver noticed and smiled broadly. "You know, I wasn't much bigger than you when I taught a Guardian to read embroidery. Asking opens the door to learning."

Ofir shared, "Cherubim *always* learn to

interpret Weavers' rows."

Darda spread his hands wide. "I had no idea. To what end?"

"Princes and captains use our stitching to quickly sort a legion by Flight, experience, and weaponry."

"May I learn?" Koji tugged Weft's sleeve. "Please?"

The Weaver smiled indulgently. "We'll talk to Cherith about adding lessons with me to your schedule. But for now, give your attention to Darda. *He* is your mentor at the moment."

"Indeed." Mimicking the older boy's own gesture, Koji spread his hands wide and recited what he'd already learned from Cherith. "I am the eyes and ears of heaven. Words are my service. Teach me to set my thoughts upon a page."

Darda's mouth twitched with amusement. "Slow down, bright eyes. Newfoundlings have to begin at the beginning."

"Reading?" Koji guessed.

"Returning."

Weathered brick. Rusted metal. Hardscrabble ground. Peaceful clucking. Koji noted the twists of wire someone had used to mend the gap demons had made in the fence. Otherwise, the chicken yard looked the same as he remembered.

"Why are we here?"

"God placed you here for a reason," explained Darda. "This is your beginning, and your first task as an Observer is to archive it."

"My beginning," Koji echoed, his attention sharpening on details he'd missed earlier. Like the dozens of windows facing the alley, each providing a different view—sagging blankets, stacked boxes, torn curtains, yellowed shades, wilting plants, and a sleeping cat.

"Put words to what your senses tell you. Trace the hand of God as it appears here." Darda patted his shoulder. "I will require a faithful record."

Koji asked, "How long do I have?"

"Evening and morning."

With a cautious look up and down the alley, he ventured, "Is it safe?"

Ofir pointed to the building opposite the chicken coop. "Darda and I will be on the roof.

The view's excellent. If there's even a whiff of mischief, I'll be at your side before you smell it."

Koji sniffed and wrinkled his nose. *Alley smells are not as nice as pollen and honey, but they are interesting.*

"Look and listen," urged Darda. "After sunrise, we will return to the tower, and you shall have pen and paper."

Long shadows cast the chicken yard into darkness by the time Koji finished his meticulous survey. But it wasn't enough. *Something is lacking.* Going up on tiptoe, the boy waved to Ofir.

The cherub wasted no time in swooping to his side. "Need something, friend?"

"I wish to see more. From above."

"I can change your perspective quick as a wink. What did you have in mind?"

From what Darda had explained, Observers

watched Creation from on high. Towers gave them a broader view of the world. Koji crossed to a scraggly tree that had more height than breadth. Hemmed in by blocks of apartment buildings, only its topmost leaves caught the angling sunlight. "That branch?"

"Kind of a puny perch. Then again, you're a featherweight." Ofir laced his fingers together, creating a foothold. "Upsie daisy!"

After a brief scramble, he thanked the cherub, who returned to his post. Koji tried several positions before settling down. One foot swinging, he sat with his other leg tucked up to his chest. Chin on knee, the young Observer gazed down at the milling chickens. *This is good. I can see farther.*

Hens were pleasant enough company, but Koji's heart leapt at the sound of shuffling footsteps. *The old woman from before!* She entered the alley carrying a single plastic bag. Leaning forward, Koji tried to catch the tune she was humming. But then she did something strange.

Walking over to a lumpish pile beside a dented garbage can, she said, "Evening,

Watchdog. There was a fine sale on tinned hash today. Bring us each an egg and we'll have an extra nice supper."

To Koji's amazement, the heap moved and stretched, transforming into a shaggy man in ragged clothes. *I did not notice him.* The oversight felt like a mistake, but he liked this turn of events. *Having people to watch is more interesting than chickens.*

"Yes'm, missus," said the man. His voice was rough, but his words were polite. "I'd like that."

While the woman creaked up her porch steps, Watchdog limped to the gate and let himself into the chicken yard. Koji held his breath until the man emerged from the coop with two eggs in one grubby hand. *He is the keeper of these chickens?*

Koji frowned in concentration as the man presented his offering at the woman's door, then sat on her porch steps. Not long afterward, she came back outside carrying two plates. The man accepted one and waited until the old woman eased into a white-painted rocker. She said grace, and they shared a meal.

Easy manners. Comfortable silences. One-sided chatting. The longer Koji eavesdropped, the more certain he was that this was their usual routine.

The woman read to her guest from grocery store fliers, discussing coupons and sale prices. "We may have to pinch pennies, but at least we have them," she said with a smile.

Watchdog ate slowly and listened close. But he didn't say anything.

Evening fell, and lights flicked on in apartment windows. Soon, the rooftops were lined with guardian angels. It reminded Koji a little of the chickens, who returned to their roosts at night. Angels lined the rooftops and chose spots on the fire escapes. *The hadarim form Hedges. Ever near those they guard.*

Gathering up the empty plates, the old woman said her good nights. "Thank you, Watchdog. If any of your friends come lookin' for a spot, make them welcome. I'll fry your eggs at breakfast."

"Yes'm, missus. Thank you for your hospitality," he gruffly replied. "Sleep sweet."

"Always do."

Her door clicked shut, and the man collected a plaid blanket from a cardboard box on the corner of her porch. Wrapping it around his shoulders, he stretched out right in front of his hostess's door. *Like a watchdog.*

Koji watched stars prickle their way into the patch of sky overhead, and he listened to the occasional rustle of feathers in the hen house below. But his gaze kept straying from the old woman's empty roof to her porch, where the homeless man dozed on her doormat.

Finally, Koji whispered, "Asking opens the door to learning."

Sliding from his branch to the roof of the chicken coop, he dropped to the ground and padded across the alley. Up the steps. Onto the porch. Koji bent over the still figure, waiting. When he didn't stir, Koji tentatively poked a whiskered cheek.

Under grizzled eyebrows, one eye opened, then the other.

Koji fidgeted under Watchdog's steady gaze. But he had come this far, and his question felt important. Keeping his voice low, Koji solemnly asked, "Why are you pretending to be a man?"

*In various times and in various ways,
the lives of men and angels have
come together on common ground.
In much the same manner as the
Redeeming Son, they are Sent
to earth to serve as men.
Or on rare occasion, as boys.*

PART FIVE
PEN AND PAPER

Watchdog slowly sat up, scratching at the side of his face as he peered at his angelic visitor. "Haven't you heard of Grafts?"

"No." Koji crouched before the homeless man. "You are a Guardian."

"I am."

"And the lady …?"

"Her name is under my hand."

The young angel looked at the door Watchdog barred. "You are her guardian angel."

"I am," he repeated. "But why are *you* here, Observer? Where's your mentor?"

Koji hesitated. *Where, indeed?* "I have many mentors."

"One mentor for one apprentice. That is the way of things."

"Then I have no mentor."

"First, it's many; now, it's none?" The Guardian took the hem of Koji's sleeve between two grimy fingers. "You're not newfound, for the Weavers have been of service. Do you have a name?"

"I have two. Maybe three. I am uncertain if 'bright eyes' counts."

Watchdog cracked a smile. "Your hidden name is for God. Nicknames are for friends. If you'll share your given name, I'll tell you what I'm called in the heavenlies."

"Ofir named me Koji."

"And is Ofir that yellow-winged cherub?"

Koji turned in the direction his companion was looking. On the roof of the apartment building across the alley, Ofir stood out against the stars. "Indeed."

When the young Protector lifted a hand, both Koji and Watchdog returned the gesture.

Koji searched for clearer words. "I am here to

learn, and you are my assignment."

Grizzled brows lifted. "You were Sent to me?"

"Not *exactly*, but I was told to seek traces of God's hand in this place." Koji solemnly explained, "You show His kindness and care to a lady who shows His kindness and care to you. It is interesting to watch."

Watchdog found a more comfortable position and patted the plank floor at his side. Once Koji accepted the invitation, the disguised angel said, "I'm usually beneath notice in these rags. People are so quick to look away, I may as well be invisible."

"Your lady sees you."

"She sees in part, but it has been enough."

Enough for what? Koji's questions were piling up. *How long have you been friends with your lady? Does a beard tickle? When did you become a keeper of chickens?* But the boy gave voice to the most urgent question first. "May I know your heavenly name?"

The Guardian straightened, and his voice smoothed out. "I am Ravel, mentor to none, apprentice to none. But by the mercy of God

Most High, my joy is full."

Koji tipped his head to one side. "Why?"

Ravel scratched thoughtfully at his bristling jaw. "Reasons unseen and hopes invisible."

I am unseen. To his lady, I would be invisible. But I do not think that is what he means. Koji tried scratching his own chin, but it didn't clarify matters. So he tried another question. "I am the eyes and ears of heaven. How can I observe the unseen and the invisible?"

"Practice." Ravel explained, "Details are one thing; impressions are another. The first takes a sharp eye, but the second needs a different kind of attention."

"Attention to things unseen?"

"You will soon understand, Observer. Humans are complex and full of contradictions. The evidence you seek for your records may play out before your eyes, but God works beneath the surface. He touches hearts and souls."

"But *I* cannot read a heart."

"There is a human saying, that some people wear their heart on their sleeve." Koji checked the embroidered cuff of his tunic, and the Guardian chuckled. "There is a faithful saying. Out of the overflow of the heart the mouth speaks."

Understanding dawned. "I will know the heart because words and deeds reveal it."

"Intentions become actions. Feelings become emotions. Faith becomes sight." Ravel said, "You will mark many intangible influences—pride, foolishness, mercy, jealousy, guilt, embarrassment, happiness. And then there is sin, which yields its terrible fruit. But there is also faith, hope, and love."

Koji's thoughts were reeling. *Visible and invisible. They are tied together. To understand what I see, I must consider what I cannot see.* The boy placed his hand on the rough cloth of Ravel's coat. "You are a good mentor."

Ravel flinched.

And Koji looked closer. "'One mentor for one apprentice. That is the way of things.' But you are Ravel, 'mentor to none, apprentice to none.'" The young Observer whispered, "What am I not seeing?"

"Old wounds. Deep scars. Lingering regrets." Ravel pushed back his overgrown hair, revealing his left ear, which was pierced by two heavy silver rings. "Everyone you meet will be more than they seem. And God plays a part in every one of their stories."

Koji scooted closer and touched the rings, then the unkempt beard. "Tell me more?"

"It's not my place to lecture Observers."

"Not a lesson." With outspread hands, Koji offered his full attention. "Let me bear witness to your story."

Just before dawn, Ofir and Darda collected Koji, leaving the angelic guard dog to his solitary post.

"Did you see many things?" Darda quizzed as they retreated down the alley.

"Indeed."

"Did you listen well?"

Koji nodded eagerly.

Ofir scooped him up and swung him around. "Were you nervous for nothing?"

The blue-winged cherub arrived to carry Darda, but Koji only had eyes for Ofir. "How did you know?"

"Keen intuition." The cherub spread his wings and climbed into the sunrise sky.

Does that not mean he observed my invisible feelings? Would Cherith let me take lessons from Ofir as well? Koji solemnly asked, "Can you teach me to sharpen my intuition?"

"Don't get the wrong idea, friend," the older boy said with a wide smile. "Wasn't so long ago I was a knock-kneed newbie. But you were brilliant. How did you single out that Graft so quick?"

"He was alone."

"That's all?"

Koji thought back. "That is why I watched him more closely. You know about Grafts?"

"Not much," Ofir replied. "Watchdog's the only one I ever heard of. And tonight's the first I ever saw him so scruffy. The day I found you, your new friend was armored, unfurled, and swinging that ax of his at the Fallen."

I learned many things about Ravel, yet there is more. Moments I missed. Stories he saved for next time. The Guardian's tale had stirred Koji's heart, and empathy made it hard for the boy to figure out which feelings were his own and which ones belonged to the story. Somehow, Koji knew that once he finished archiving Ravel's history, his thoughts would be his own again. But they would be changed because he'd met an angel called Watchdog.

Darda led Koji into a small alcove near the top of the tower. Rapping his knuckles on the small desk that stood at its center, he said, "Make yourself comfortable, bright eyes. This is your niche."

"Mine?" Koji caressed the desk's smooth wood before sliding onto its bench. His feet didn't quite reach the floor, so they swung in time with the giddy beating of his heart. "Thank you!"

Stocked drawers. Odd nooks. Surprising crannies. Koji was eager to get to know his work space, but Darda went on. "Paper is here. Ink will go here once you are ready for it. But beginners start with these." He flipped open the lid on a box of slim chalks. "Prosper has you next, and he will make sure your rows are legible. But for now, I will help you organize your thoughts."

Tapping the edge of the soft-hued colors,

Koji asked, "May I use these?"

Darda chuckled. "Go for it, bright eyes! Every Observer's fingers itch to create."

"Yours, too?"

The older boy wiggled his fingers, "Always. But my easel will be there. You are my first concern."

"We could share," Koji shyly offered.

No other persuasion was needed. Both angels were soon sprawled on the floor, heads bent over their artwork. The lesson touched on everything from recognizing pivotal moments to blending the powdery chalk to achieve a wider range of colors.

Koji was admiring Darda's rooftop pigeon portraits when one of the other Observers rushed in. "Have you heard?"

"Doubtful. I am recently returned."

"Cherith has gone to collect an Observer. He will return soon!"

Darda quickly sat up. "Another newfoundling? Or a mentor?"

"An Observer in need of an apprentice." In awed tones, the other boy added, "And not just *any* potential mentor. Shimron is a First One!"

Angels may live without end,
but there is only One
with no beginning and no end.
Every angel remembers
his beginning. And among the
vast hosts of heaven,
there are those who remember
Time's beginning. These oldest of
angels are known as the First.

PART SIX
FIRST AND FOREMOST

Prosper left off pacing to inspect Koji's rows. Touching his pupil's shoulder, he said, "While your mind is muddling, your ink is puddling."

Koji jerked to attention and dropped his pen, scattering more blots across his practice sheet. "Sorry," he mumbled, trying to brush aside his mistake. The spots only smeared, further ruining the page.

"Haste and waste." Prosper rescued Koji's roll-away pen and capped the pot of indigo ink. Bumping the boy over, he joined Koji on the bench. "Where have you been wandering? The path must have been pleasant to have beguiled you so completely."

Scooting over to make more room, Koji offered a meek shrug. "I do not think I could retrace the course. One question brings three more." Prosper didn't seem upset by his lapse, and that made it easier to admit, "There is still so much I do not know."

"Do not bottle up ignorance like ink. Spill out your questions, and I will turn them into answers."

Koji searched the older boy's bright blue eyes and found a playful sparkle that stirred his curiosity. So he asked the question that was foremost in his mind. "What *is* a First One?"

Prosper chose a brush and opened a small paint pan. Loading its bristles with luminous color, he explained, "The First are angels who bore witness to Creation. They are older than Time. And from among their number, God set apart princes."

"Princes?"

"The archangels." Prosper turned Koji's parchment sideways and connected several ink spots. A smear became part of a prince's crisscrossing sash.

Koji asked, "Is Shimron an archangel?"

"No." Trading his brush for the pen, Prosper chose the same ink Koji had been using earlier. "But Shimron is treated with unusual deference by the cherub who arrived with him."

"Perhaps they are friends."

Prosper shook his head. "Unless Weft is teasing, that Protector is his captain."

Koji had noticed the angel in question, a stern-faced cherub with green wings. "That is as it should be. Flights are given to the cherubim."

"But the adahim are not given to Flights. Not *usually*."

"We serve in towers."

"Ever on high." Prosper lapsed into silence as he worked a pair of cherubim into his design. And Koji watched with increasing admiration as calligraphy framed a glorious throne. Colors blended softly, and a poem spiraled outward.

In one corner of the transformed page, Prosper drew a little boy kneeling at the base of a white tower. Ink-stained hands folded over his heart as he opened his mouth. *This is the me that Prosper sees.* Koji whispered, "I like to sing."

"Your songs are sweet."

When Prosper finally set aside his tools, Koji's mess was a masterpiece. The boy asked, "Can I learn to make beautiful things like you?"

"No."

Koji pouted.

Prosper smiled. "No, for *your* record will have a beauty only *you* can add. One as beguiling as the faraway stars in your eyes."

Words failed the little wordsmith, so Koji swallowed hard and flung his arms around Prosper.

The older boy laughed, then sighed. Sifting his fingers through Koji's hair, Prosper said, "Sweet as honey, innocent as flowers. Was I ever as new as you?"

Holding tight, Koji dared to ask another question. "Will you go with Shimron if he chooses you?"

"If choice was truly mine, I would rather be bound to you."

Koji looked up and wondered what it would be like, having Prosper for his own. With a regretful headshake, he said, "I was not Sent to you."

"Yet here you are." Prosper kissed his forehead, then firmly said, "And here you shall *stay* until you fill a fresh page with rows."

As Cherith's rotation sent Koji from one mentor to the next, he learned more about the life he'd been created for. Student. Historian. Illustrator. Shelver. He pushed one last chronicle into its place. "I am finished," he reported.

His latest mentor released him with a grateful nod. "Weft has you next."

Finally! Although Koji appreciated each of his many teachers, he loved coming full circle. Running until his feet met the plush carpet that marked Weft's tower-top domain, he called, "I am here!"

Yahavim whirled down from the potted candle-trees, humming excitedly, and their shepherd welcomed him warmly. "Prompt as ever. Are you still eluding the First One?"

"Somehow." The boy accepted manna from Weft's flock, then hurried to sit with him. "Even at evensong, I have not come close enough to see the color of his eyes."

"And no wonder, with eager prospects pressing in on all sides. The whole tower conspires to keep you from meeting Shimron."

"I do not mind so much. You have made it a game."

"One you are enjoying?"

"Indeed."

The Weaver spread a six-fingered hand wide. "Then by all means begin. What have you learned about our elusive guest?"

Koji solemnly reported, "Shimron has mastered every form of artistry known to heaven, but he favors painting with the light of rainbows."

"Is such a thing even possible?"

"I do not see how, but it is a pleasing thought."

"Granted. What else?"

"Shimron has a tower all to himself."

"True!"

Koji blinked. He'd expected that to be another exaggeration. *Would having a tower to yourself be lonely? It almost sounds like a prison.* "Shimron carries an inkhorn, the mark of a traveler. But no one seems to know where he has been or where he is going."

"True! And truly mysterious." Weft's smile grew wider as he made his own contribution. "Shimron is fond of yahavim and often stops by to visit my flock."

"I had not heard th–"

A soft voice interrupted. "True."

Koji's eyes widened as an angel with snow-white hair stepped out from behind one of the chamber's many embroidered curtains. Darda was with him, all smiles as he escorted their guest forward.

Weft asked, "Surprised?"

"Indeed."

Shimron said, "Everywhere I hear rumors of a newfoundling, and every evensong, his voice soars high and sweet. Yet I have not come close enough to see the color of his eyes."

Koji quickly stood and took the hand Shimron offered. Without really meaning to, the boy began to catalog the person before him. Confirming some rumors, casting out others. And making up his own mind on several points. *His smile is kind. His touch is light. His voice is gentle.* And one lingering mystery was finally solved. "Your eyes are blue."

Shimron replied with equal gravity. "And yours are brown."

Weft explained, "Shimron and I have business to discuss, so we'll postpone your lesson. I trust you won't mind skipping straight to Darda?"

Koji nodded distractedly, for his attention was caught by hints of unseen things.

Shimron asked, "Lessons with a Weaver?"

"I'm one of Koji's many mentors," said Weft. "He's been learning to read stitching."

Darda teased, "Mind your cuffs if you want to keep any secrets."

A cherub dropped into the room with a rush of green wings. He folded powerful arms over his chest and demanded, "Who *else* has learned the Weavers' rows?"

"Only Koji." Weft stepped up behind the boy and clapped a hand over his eyes. "And he's not looking."

"I looked," Koji said. *And not just at his cuffs. It is just as Ravel said. Every person is more than they seem.*

The cherub sighed. "And what did you see, little Observer?"

Koji obediently reported, "You are Jedrick, captain of the Flight to which Shimron belongs. The names of his *current* teammates are Abner, Padgett, Harken, Milo, Myr–"

"Stop," Jedrick snapped. "How much of Shimron's history you read?"

"Only what is here."

"*Only*," Weft muttered, removing his hand.

Koji looked way, *way* up into the Protector's unhappy face. "But something is missing."

Jedrick grumbled something about precautions.

Tipping his head to one side, Koji searched

Shimron's startled face. *It is there. Down deep. He hides the same things as Ravel. Regret. Sorrow. Pain.* Ignoring the narrowed gaze of the looming cherub, Koji slipped his arms around Shimron's neck and held on until the ancient angel returned his embrace.

A catch. A tremor. And Koji knew he was right. But he didn't know the reason. So he asked. "Why are you so sad?"

*When the first to Fall was cast
from heaven, one third
of the angels followed him
into exile. Those who
remained Faithful witnessed
sin's penalty, so when
newfoundlings were added to
their number, the First Ones
took them to their hearts
as apprentices and warned
them against Satan's folly.
God alone is Most High.*

PART SEVEN
HIGH AND MIGHTY

When six cherubim sailed through the passage Cherith had made back into the created world, the sun was low in the west, but Koji quickly lost sight of the setting star. Lightning flickered an instant before the cherub dropped through heavy clouds, dousing them both.

Cold! And wet! Koji squinted against the spatter of raindrops, enjoying the new sensation. *This is how the earth is washed and watered. Like a bath that is poured out.*

But when they reached the now familiar alley, things were far from clean. Dirt bled across cracked asphalt, collecting in slimy puddles. Grimy water splashed Koji's legs as Ofir set him down and loosened his spear in one smooth motion. "Careful!" the young Protector shouted to their companions.

Yellow wings drew close, offering a sun-bright shelter from the sheeting rain. Koji's nose wrinkled at the putrid smell hanging in the air. A howl ripped through the murk, and he understood. *There are Fallen nearby.* The alley had once more become a battlefield.

Koji's hands locked around Ofir's arm.

"Hey, hey, hey now. I'm right here."

"And Darda?"

Ofir let his wing dip enough so they could check. Koji's current mentor knelt beside his own escort, peering intently through the rain. Raising his voice, Ofir called, "Darda! High-tail it!"

The jade-haired Observer immediately broke cover, and Koji helped pull him to safety. Darda flicked at dripping braids and dredged up a smile. "Sorry, bright eyes. Cherith didn't mention anything about a fracas. Are you okay?"

"Indeed."

Once released from shielding Darda, the

blue-winged cherub drew his sword and followed the others into the fray. "Turns out we're reinforcements!" Ofir leaned forward, and a slow smile spread across his face. "Eyes forward, Observer. My buddies are backing up a friend of yours!"

Ravel? Koji pushed wet bangs out of his eyes and searched the gray haze, but there was no sign of a scruffy beggar. Big and broad, with red wings flung wide, a singular warrior towered over the rest. Bronze hair clung to his face as he slashed a broad arc with a double-bladed ax. Would anyone believe that this was the same person? But Koji couldn't look away. *There is no doubt. He is my friend. Watchdog.*

In the soggy aftermath of a short-lived battle, Koji trotted across the emptying alley, darting between the legs of other warriors in his hurry to get to Ravel. The Guardian was much taller than when he was in human guise, so Koji had to stretch on tiptoe to reach his hand.

Ravel started, his eyes widening slightly.

"*You* were here?"

"I bore witness to your battle! You are truly one of God's mighty ones!"

"And *you* are ill-equipped to defend yourself." To Koji's surprise, Ravel scooped him up, tucking him into the crook of one muscular arm and draping him with the trailing edge of his wing. "Show more caution, Observer."

"Ofir is with me." Koji pointed at the opposite rooftop and amended, "*Was* with me."

"Then I shall be your shelter."

Koji peered over the swathe of vivid crimson. "Is the enemy gone?"

"For the moment." Ravel strode to the porch and sat with his back to the door. His usual post. Propping his ax against the wall, Ravel shook the rain from hair that hung in waves around his shoulders. "He may return. He always does."

"Who?"

The Guardian's half-smile was all sadness. "You know my story. Venture a guess."

Koji tipped his head to one side, trying to put this attack into perspective. *Ravel is apprentice to none because his charge died, mentor to none because his apprentice Fell. Twice-pierced. Now a Graft. Standing guard over the woman whose name remains under his hand.* The pieces slipped into place. Koji stirred and asked, "The one who was your apprentice. Does he remember your lady?"

Ravel tucked his chin and sighed. "Remembers *and* loves, although sin has twisted his affection into horrible shapes."

Reaching up, Koji touched the Guardian's smooth face. Without a beard to hide his emotions, the invisible was much easier to see. "Will you tell me the part you held back?"

He shook his head. "I do not want to fill your ears with ugliness."

"I wish to make a faithful record. How did your apprentice Fall?"

"Little by little, and all at once."

And so Ravel spoke through the night. Haltingly at first. Retracing the downward spiral that had landed him on this rickety porch with a flock of chickens and a nickname.

"You could not have prevented it." Koji meant it as reassurance, but Ravel took it as a question.

"I have asked myself that very thing many

times." With a faraway look in his eyes, the Guardians said, "There were little things. Small changes. From time to time, he would say or do something that should have warned me."

"Like what?"

"Passing remarks. Baseless suspicions. Veiled insults. He avoided my gaze, and his ears grew dull. Toward the end, his wings were silent, and he abandoned evensong. Then food started disappearing from our charge's household— sugar cubes, candy, and jellies."

"He stole sweets?" Koji asked.

"By the time I realized that he was dimming from lack of manna, heaven's guards arrived to cast him out. It was over before I fully realized what had begun." Ravel heaved a shuddering sigh. "I was blind."

"Only God sees the heart."

Ravel nodded once. "And only God knows when it has shattered beyond repair."

Words were whirling through Koji's mind when he traded dawn's pink sky for meadows of golden flowers. Ofir returned to his post and Darda to his easel, but the boy meandered toward the crystal stream. For a while, he simply watched the water ripple over smooth white stones. Ordering his thoughts. Settling on a sequence. Preparing to set Ravel's record on a page.

But Koji's sharp ears picked up an unfamiliar sound. *A chorus of bees?* Curious why his peaceable neighbors were swarming, the boy followed the stream away from the tower. At regular intervals, he passed squat columns, the hives Cherith maintained. Pressing his ear to each, Koji caught the sleepy drone of contented bees. *Not here either.* The discord was coming from further down the row.

He waded carefully through nodding flowers. Silky petals. Spicy pollen. Koji's nose twitched, and he quickly covered it, for voices reached him.

" ...missing. And you know what it could mean."

That was Cherith. Koji recognized the next speaker as the cherub called Jedrick.

"Too well. Are there no mentors here?"

"Middlings, one and all. Perhaps Shimron

will be able t– "

Koji crouched down, burying his face in his hands, but it was no use. Sneezing like a newfoundling, he gave himself away.

"You!" exclaimed Cherith.

Koji peeked up and went cross-eyed, staring at the point of Jedrick's sword.

With a huff, the cherub re-sheathed his weapon, then offered his hand. "Peace, child. You have nothing to fear."

"Indeed," he said, rubbing at his itching, twitching nose. "But the bees …?"

"Fear not. I will calm them." Cherith dropped to his knees and opened his arms to Koji. "I hear you made quite an impression on Shimron."

I speak of bees; he speaks of guests? Although he gratefully accepted the hug, Koji ignored the change of subject. "Are they afraid?"

After a lengthy pause, the Caretaker sat back on his heels. "Frantic. And furious. Someone meddled with their hive."

Cherith said something is missing. That's why the bees are angry. Uneasiness slipped into Koji's heart, for Ravel's story was still fresh in his mind. And he didn't like the direction his thoughts were taking. "Not *here*."

"What is not here?" Jedrick asked.

Koji began to tremble. "Is it too late?"

Cherith's voice turned soft and solemn. "Why are you so fraught, young one?"

"It is said that the bread of angels tastes as if God first dipped it in honey!" Koji recited. He grabbed fistfuls of Cherith's raiment. "Did someone take honey?"

*When God places a newfoundling
into the keepingof an older, wiser angel,
He gives two gifts at once. For
while it's true that apprentices are
given to their mentors, each mentor
is also given to his apprentice.
Some pairings are harder to
understand than others, but
without fail, God gives good gifts.*

PART EIGHT
GIVE AND TAKE

Cherith's expression buckled into bewilderment. "What would you know about that?"

Sweet things. Small changes. Koji tried to hide behind the heavy curtain of the Caretaker's roped hair.

"What have you seen?" he asked. "What do you know?"

"Is it too late?"

"No." Jedrick's voice was closer, for he was kneeling now. The warrior added, "Not all who waver Fall."

"If the honey is gone, that is bad," Koji said.

"Ravel told me."

"*That* explains it." Cherith spoke over Koji's head. "He managed to befriend a twice-pierced, grafted Guardian."

"Do you realize how extraordinarily *rare* …?"

Cherith's eyebrows arched. "I have seen enough rarities to understand their worth. As have you."

Jedrick grumbled softly.

Have I displeased him? Koji glanced back again, but Jedrick didn't seem upset. In fact, he'd spread his wings, offering shelter. Maybe this cherub could help. "You are new."

"The time when I was newfound is long past," said Jedrick.

Shaking his head, Koji tried for better words. "A dimming angel hides in his friends' blind spot. But you are new to this place. You can look *and* see."

Jedrick nodded once.

Koji turned in Cherith's arms to face the cherub. "It is not too late?"

"No," Jedrick repeated. "God draws many back to Himself."

"How?"

"In as many ways as there are needs."

Hope unfurled in Koji's heart, but Cherith said, "I have bees to tend. Go with Jedrick."

Jedrick stood. "I will take you to Shimron."

Koji hesitated, and Cherith explained, "Everyone in the tower is laying aside their work. A pair of Worshipers is newly arrived. They are here to lead us in song. And perhaps to create an opportunity."

"I thought of that as well," said Jedrick.

Opportunity?

Before Koji could ask what they meant, Jedrick took Koji by the shoulder. "Come along, little Observer. Shimron will be watching for you."

Koji followed the Protector away from the hives, trotting to keep up. Once Koji could no longer hear the angry buzz of bees, he asked, "Opportunity?"

Jedrick slowed his steps. "When an angel cannot find peace, he should seek out a Worshiper. The zamarim bear witness to broken hearts and barren hopes. They can lead the wavering back into worship."

"That is good."

The Protector's stern features softened. "May the one who is suffering reach out and grasp hope."

Koji nodded and glanced around, for they'd reached the assembly.

"You found him!" Shimron exclaimed, but with one look into Koji's face, his smile faded. The First One quietly asked, "Captain?"

"Later," Jedrick said, excusing himself with a nod.

Shimron guided Koji through the gathering. His hand on the boy's back was the only thing keeping him moving. *I want to leave. I do not want to see.* Still, Koji's gaze darted from side to side, automatically cataloging the attendees.

What would happen if someone was missing?

Whispers rippled through the middling Observers, and at first Koji paid no attention. But to his relief, everyone in the tower was present. *There is hope,* he reminded himself.

Finally, stray remarks caught his attention. A hint here. A guess there. They were saying that Shimron's choice was made, and Koji's heart sank. Didn't that mean he'd be leaving soon? *Which of my teachers will go with him?* Koji searched the crowd, trying to guess who had found the First One's favor, but something was strange. *Why are they all looking at me?*

"Koji?" murmured Shimron. "What is wrong?"

He chose an answer that fit both problems. "I do not want to lose any of my mentors."

The oddest expression flitted across the ancient angel's face. "And I do not wish to lose any apprentices."

One of the Worshipers began a simple call to worship. Koji sang, but his whole heart wasn't in the song. Ever since Shimron's arrival, he'd spent each evensong watching the First One and making guesses about him. But now that he was at Shimron's side, his perspective widened. *How do dimming angels hide? I have been blind, but I want to see. Where is the one who needs hope?*

All of the sudden, Koji's voice failed. Breath and song left him, leaving nothing but a terrible certainty. His soul keened, and yet he couldn't look away from the one other angel who wasn't singing. He mouthed a line here and there, enough to fit in. Until his gaze locked with Koji's, and his smile faded.

In that moment, the boy felt the enormity of God's sorrow.

Shimron turned to see why Koji wasn't singing and gasped, "What is this?"

How do I answer? Koji wasn't sure what … or why … or when. Only that something needed to be done. Soon.

Shimron touched his face, catching tears with his thumb. "I do not think the song has moved you."

Koji glanced back across the gathering, but the other angel was gone. It was all the confirmation he needed. *He is the one. But why did it have to be him*? The enormity of what was happening crashed down around his heart, which broke into sobs.

Shimron's noise of surprise was quickly followed by an embrace. Fingers sifted through Koji's hair, and under cover of song, the First One's gentle voice reached his ear. "Why are you so sad?"

Koji couldn't find his voice after that. He stayed very still, taking what comfort he could from Shimron's presence. But the tightness in his throat was frightening. He opened his mouth, but no sound passed his lips. Even the whimper in his soul couldn't make it past the sudden silence. He pushed a fearful babble of thoughts toward Cherith, who would know what to do, but the Caretaker's voice didn't answer. *Am I alone?*

Lifting his face to gaze at Shimron, Koji formed a clearer question in his mind. *Can you hear me?*

The old angel glanced down with an expression of gentle concern. "Can you tell me why the stars are gone from your eyes?"

A small headshake was all the answer Koji could give. *I am alone.*

'Are you?'

Koji's heart leapt at the sound of his Maker's voice, and he waited breathlessly to hear God's plan. For what else could this be?

'When the time is right for words, you will have them.'

Koji's eyes slipped shut, and in the light behind his eyelids, God spoke kindly. *'For his sake. For your sake. And for hers. You will understand in time.'*

Hers? The boy squeezed his eyes more tightly shut and hoped for more. But the watches came and went, and the singing ended. Koji was glad to see the Worshipers join the crowd of Observers who returned to the tower. He was even happier when Ofir brought Cherith.

Shimron said, "Something is amiss. Can you help him?"

The Caretaker took one look into Koji's eyes and snorted lightly. "Who can undo what God Most High has done?"

Ofir's grim expression melted into a relieved smile. He messed up Koji's hair and said, "As long as you haven't forgotten how to smile, I won't worry."

Koji didn't want to disappoint his first friend, so he tapped his own forehead.

"You remember how?" asked Ofir, his smile widening at Koji's adamant nod.

Cherith took charge. "Shimron, this would be a good time to speak."

"It is? Ah. So be it." The First One took Koji's hand and asked, "Do you know why I am here?"

Everyone knew. He had come in search of an apprentice. Koji dipped his head.

"God has declared that the journey is too much for me, and I should not be alone." Shimron's smile was small and sad. "I have no desire to take anyone else into danger, yet … I *must* choose."

Koji's head tipped to one side. *He does not want this.*

With a sigh, Shimron said, "I *need* you, Koji. Please, write your name on my heart."

*Angels want for nothing, for God
has given them life and light.
They belong to heaven—clothed
in raiment, nurtured by manna,
dwelling in the tents and tenements
of a never-ending city. Yet angels
understand wanting. A Guardian
wants strength. A Messenger
wants words. A Worshiper wants
harmony. But sometimes angels
fashion new desires for themselves,
and in chasing after them, they
lose their way home.*

PART NINE
RIGHT AND WRONG

Silence was strange. Koji felt as if God had picked him up and set him at a distance from the others. He could see Shimron's grief like a shadow in his eyes, and Ofir's wings twitched with uneasiness. He could hear Cherith's gravity, and there was an unexpected gentleness underlying Jedrick's comments. But Koji had lost an invisible connection.

The sensation brought to mind a speckled feather he'd found on the ground in Watchdog's chicken coop. Once part of a hen, the feather had lost its place. It was definitely still a feather. He'd touched its delicate edge, admiring its design. But the fallen feather's usefulness had ended. *Is that what it means to Fall? To see, to hear, to remember ... but to be alone?*

'You are not alone. Neither is he.'

"Koji?" Shimron touched his shoulder and asked, "Can you answer?"

He pressed fingertips to his sealed lips in a silent plea for understanding.

Cherith spoke on his behalf. "Be patient, Shimron. Koji's next words do not belong to us. They are set apart for another."

"So be it." Without pushing for more, Shimron used his sleeve to dry Koji's tears. "In my experience, newfoundlings have boundless curiosity and a gift for giggling. Yet you understand sadness."

Koji nodded. Hadn't he witnessed Ravel's, taking it into himself so he could write the twice-pierced Guardian's record? And God's sorrow for the lost sang softly through his mind, stirring a lament in his own soul.

Shimron asked, "Is that why you could tell I was sad?"

Reaching up, Koji touched Shimron's cheek and offered a small nod. Sorrow didn't need to be written in tears to be legible. *Is seeing the same as understanding?* Koji wished he could ask. A First One might know.

"Other than the Guardians, few in heaven have been pierced by sadness. Yet here you are, and I have found you."

Koji pinched his left earlobe. *Am I pierced, even though I do not have an earring? Why do hadarim and adahim have different traditions if our feelings are the same? Does piercing hurt more than sadness?*

Looking to Cherith, Shimron said, "I would like to meet Koji's Guardian friend. The one known as Watchdog."

Cherith inclined his head. "A way will be made."

Shimron didn't shy away from the grizzled beggar who waited in the darkening alley. Stepping lightly across crumbling asphalt, the barefoot angel greeted Watchdog with a lengthy embrace. "Your faithfulness has touched my life through Koji. Thank you."

Watchdog shook his shaggy head. "Let the thanks go to God."

Koji slipped to the big Guardian's side and patted the trailing end of the new scarf looped around his shoulders. *Did the old woman knit it? Does Ravel like wearing something as red as his wings? Is this hospitality toward angels?* Unable to ask, Koji stored up his questions for later.

Shimron said, "Ever since I learned that you and Koji have been spending time together, I have wanted to meet you. You see, there are several Grafts in my Flight."

Koji's eyes widened. Although Shimron's stitching revealed the names of his teammates, this was news.

"Several?" Watchdog beckoned for them to join him on the porch steps. "In all my years at this post, I never met another Graft."

"Until now." Shimron touched his chest.

"There was a time when I mingled with mankind."

Shimron did? Few angels lived as men, yet Koji sat between two of them. His awe increased with every skip of his heart.

Watchdog leaned forward. "Then you understand."

"Better than most, but not entirely. You see, my friend *knew* my true nature."

"*Friend*," the Guardian echoed. "You revealed yourself?"

Shimron shook his head. "There was no need. That man was a prophet; his eyes and ears were opened by God."

Koji's questions piled up. *Is it possible for angels and humans to become friends? How did Shimron meet this prophet? Were they friends right away, or was the man frightened? Do all Grafts grow beards?* Try as he might to picture the First One with hair on his chin, Koji's imagination fell short.

Shimron backed up closer to the story's beginning. "When Time was much newer, I was Sent from my tower to the opanim. I had no need of weapons, but heaven's armorers created this."

He withdrew a curving inkhorn from beneath his sash and showed it to Ravel. "From that moment to this, it has never run dry."

Although rumors had reached Koji's ears, this was the boy's first glimpse of the ornate silver flask that fit neatly into Shimron's palm. *The mark of a traveler. God provided for his journey.* A new idea came to Koji. *If he is part of a Flight, has his journey not yet ended?*

Ravel turned it over in his hands. "A useful gift for an archivist."

Taking back the opanim's gift, Shimron uncapped the inkhorn and glanced around. "Koji, bring me a feather?"

The boy trotted over to the chicken coop and soon returned with the requested item. Shimron produced a small book with blank pages, and Koji watched in silent wonderment as the other Observer deftly turned the seemingly purposeless cast-off into a quill.

A dip. A tap. A dab. As the makeshift pen scratched across paper, Shimron said, "Like Koji, I came into the created world expecting to stand apart and watch the hand of God at work in the lives of humanity."

Koji edged closer as Shimron captured an impression with a few lines, then nurtured the spare sketch into an illustration.

The First One continued, "I was pleased to be wrong. And humbled to realize that I, too, was under the hand of God. He had a part for me to play in the life of a man whose faith was flagging."

As Shimron's story unfolded, Koji's heart beat faster. *Can I truly become his apprentice? How long would it take me to learn everything he knows?* Any of the middlings in the tower would have rejoiced to sit here and watch Shimron work. Koji wished he could share this moment with Darda, Prosper, and the others. But another desire wrestled past the generous impulse. *Mine. I want to be the one to learn from Shimron.*

The sudden surge of ambition unsettled Koji. *Is it wrong to want something so badly?* He caught the trailing end of Shimron's sleeve, which was heavy with embroidery. *Stitch my name here. Choose me for his apprentice. Let my answer be yes.* But God's hand was still over his mouth, and Koji remembered why. Hunching his shoulders, he tugged at his left earlobe.

Watchdog noticed. In a twinkling, the shabby beggar vanished, and Ravel's unfurled wing settled protectively around Koji's shoulders. His friend couldn't shield him from the pain of sorrow, but Koji found comfort in his sympathy. Ravel understood. Better than most.

When they returned to the tower, Shimron gazed across golden meadows and said, "Amazing."

Koji nodded, for the view was indeed beautiful.

"I meant you."

Dark eyes blinked. *I am a source of amazement?*

Shimron's glance held a smile. "You befriended a Graft. Your first record is fraught with his sorrow, yet remains sweet. You have learned much in a short time thanks to your middling mentors, yet you possess depths that cannot be taught. You tempt me to believe that God made you just for me, yet He keeps me in suspense as to your answer." Setting a hand atop Koji's head, he mused, "Do you suppose it is wrong to want something so badly?"

Startled to hear his own question spoken aloud, Koji flung his arms around Shimron.

"Ah." The ancient angel's embrace was as gentle as his voice. "I am reassured. The gifts from God's hand are always good. Yet one thing you lack."

Koji's head popped up, and he searched Shimron's smiling face.

"Your many mentors sing your praises in every area save one. Penmanship."

Flushing, Koji nodded. *I am still clumsy.*

"Your next lesson is with Prosper, is it not?"
Oh.

"None can deny his mastery over pen and ink. Let his skill guide you." When Shimron tried to step back, Koji clung, but the First One spoke with quiet authority. "Prosper will be waiting. Go to him while you can."

*Eternity and Time do not proceed
in the same manner. They
overlap and double back, with
hints and echoesof what could be
... and of what cannot be undone.
A Caretaker's door bridges any gap,
smoothing away contradictions, for
Time itself bends to the will of God.*

PART TEN
Lost and Found

Koji trotted obediently up the curving stairway, but Prosper wasn't at his desk.

Leaning out of a neighboring niche, Darda waved with his paintbrush. "Need something, bright eyes?"

The boy mutely indicated the empty alcove.

"If you want Prosper, check windows and ledges." With a twirl of his finger, Darda explained, "We often find him scribbling away in lofty corners."

Koji continued up his winding course, peeking into each nook and finding new crannies. The Observers' tower was certainly spacious, but there was an end to possibilities. He found Prosper a few steps shy of Weft's domain, sitting in the deep ledge of a narrow window.

Gentle breezes teased at Prosper's hair, as if trying to get his attention, but the older boy's eyes were fixed upon his book. Koji did not wait with the wind. Reaching out, he brushed white knuckles.

Prosper stirred and switched his stare to Koji's face. Eyebrows lifting, he asked, "You want your lesson?"

An earnest nod.

If Prosper thought his silence strange, he didn't say so. "I am comfortable and do not wish to leave this spot. Bring your things to me."

But when Koji returned with an armload of supplies, Prosper had abandoned his perch.

This time, the boy's search spiraled downward. Bare feet padded along balconies and between bookshelves until he found Prosper sitting idly at an unassigned desk. Koji placed a neat bundle at his elbow—paper, pen, and ink.

"What of paints?" asked Prosper.

Koji tipped his head to one side. He couldn't answer. Neither could he ask if paints were needed for a lesson in penmanship. But he left to retrieve his tray of colors and a brush.

Once again, Koji found an empty seat. His supplies remained on the desk, and the topmost page bore a message in Prosper's handwriting.

> **Don't follow**
> **one hollow;**
> **I'll wallow**
> **ALONE.**

He is wrong. We were never meant to be alone. Koji touched the message's final flourish, which was new enough for the ink to stain his fingertips. Prosper's lettering was unrivaled in beauty, but those seven words said something terrible. The contrast drove Koji's thoughts in an interesting direction. *He knows I must follow. And now I know how he feels. Will that help me help him?*

Sliding onto the borrowed bench, Koji uncapped his ink bottle and dipped his pen. His hand shook, but his response was still legible. *If beautiful writing can be bleak, can messy writing be hope?* Koji supposed it must be true. Why else would God ask him to try?

He found Prosper at the very top of the tower, sitting on the floor behind one of Weft's potted trees. There was no sign of the Weaver, but his flock of yahavim were busy in the candle-tree branches.

As Koji stole closer to Prosper's hiding place, he caught the scratch of a pen. Words flowed across one page and onto the next. Koji wondered at their meaning, but before he could read any part, Prosper closed his book with a snap.

"Is this a game? Or am *I* your game?" His voice took on a sing-song quality. "Hated, haunted, hunted."

Koji shook his head. This was obedience … and a shining droplet of hope.

"Little fool." Prosper balled his hands into fists. "Why seek what you do not want to find?"

Again, Koji shook his head. Gently working his fingers under Prosper's clenched ones, he pressed a fold of paper against his palm. *These are my next words, and they belong to you.*

Prosper skimmed the scanty lines, and pain registered on his face. Pushing Koji aside, he fled, but not far. Prosper bolted across the room, tore one of Weft's tapestries from the wall, and crawled under it. As if hiding from Koji's hope. Perhaps even from God.

Is this ... shame? Crossing to the crumpled wall hanging, Koji lifted a trailing edge and gasped when Prosper snatched his wrist and dragged him under.

"Foolish. Mulish. Meddling Nettling."

Since Weft wove with light, they weren't in the dark, but the close, muffled space was nothing like a sheltering wing. *We are hidden. Will we speak of hidden things?*

Blue eyes glittered with unshed tears. "Why must you pry?"

Koji blinked.

Thrusting the note under the boy's nose, Prosper asked, "Do you want me so much? Would you keep me if you could?"

If I could? Even if Koji could have spoken, he wasn't sure how to answer.

Prosper laughed softly. "You are wise not to answer. *If* is a sad condition for those with no choice."

But there was a choice. An important one. So Koji pulled him close and kissed his forehead, just as Prosper had done once before. "Stay." His silence broken, Koji repeated his clumsily written message. "You are my precious friend. *Stay*."

Prosper hugged him so tightly, it hurt. "If Shimron chooses you, will you go?"

"An angel goes where he is Sent."

"Go then. Run fast. Run far. Run away. *Or ....*" Prosper gentled both his grip and his tone. "Run away with me. Am I not your friend? Be faithful to me, and the bleak will be less lonesome."

Koji pushed back enough to search Prosper's face. "This is where I belong. This is where you belong."

"Neither of us belongs here anymore."

Tears welling, Koji asked, "Why?"

A tremor. A tightening. A tense whisper. "I wonder."

"No," he moaned.

But Prosper wasn't listening. He narrowed his eyes and complained, "You are too bright for me."

From somewhere behind them, a shout rang out. With a yank, the tapestry vanished. Prosper shied away from a shrill whirlwind of yahavim, hiding his face against Koji's shoulder.

"Hey, hey, hey, now. This is no place for you to be." Ofir carefully pried him from Prosper's hold. Koji wanted to protest, but the cherub's expression was so fierce.

Ofir tugged, and Koji's fingers slipped. Hauled back. Passed along. Held apart. A confusion of bronze feathers and bared weapons was the last thing Koji saw before Jedrick carried him down the stairs, out the tower door, and into the meadow beyond.

Will they save him? Were they Sent to help? Koji twisted in the cherub's grasp.

But Jedrick caught his chin and sternly said, "You have seen more than enough. Do not look back."

So Koji went limp. And looked forward.

"Have you found your voice?"

"Yes." Koji tore his gaze from the expanse of glittering stars to check Jedrick's face. The grim cherub had walked to the end of golden meadows, then leapt from heaven's threshold into darkness. Until now, Koji's only view of the stars had been a thin strip between the tall buildings in Ravel's alley. But Jedrick carried him through a vast expanse where galaxies wheeled past shimmering nebula. *I am part of this sky. I shine with the hosts. But Prosper's light ....*

"Do you have questions?"

Koji poked a finger into the decorative edging on Jedrick's armor. Questions were piling up, but asking them would force him to bear their answers. And they would be heavy. *Can I run from them—fast, far, and away?* Searching

Jedrick's face, he asked, "How far can you fly?"

"As far as you need."

The answer comforted Koji. *I could not outrun them alone. Is this mercy?*

"Since you will not ask, I will tell." Jedrick announced, "Your name has come under my hand. God has placed you under my protection."

"How can that be?" Koji's gaze slid to the cuff on Jedrick's left ear. "You are a cherub."

"As is my apprentice. He is the youngest in my Flight. Until now. I am your captain."

"Captain," Koji repeated, testing the word. "I am in a Flight."

Even though it wasn't really a question, Jedrick answered, "Yes."

"And Shimron is my mentor."

"I am glad for his sake. And for yours." Jedrick's expression wavered. "You are trembling."

"I am the eyes and ears of heaven, and I am full of words." Koji drew a shaky breath, then gravely announced. "I must sing a song of endings. Are we far?"

"As close as you need," assured Jedrick.

Immediately, a way opened, and the created

world lay below. Moonlight reflected off a pond and revealed orderly rows of fruit trees. Guardians arrayed buildings and borderlines. And for a fleeting moment, Koji glimpsed light shining from a window with diamond panes of colored glass.

Jedrick drew his attention to the white tower rising above an encampment. "You are so new, you may not yet have learned the truth about endings."

As they swooped lower, Koji considered the odd assortment of angels waiting at the base of Shimron's tower. A burly warrior with a yahavim sitting on his head. A redhead wearing a tie dyed T-shirt and flip-flops. A park ranger with braids and a bandana. And an elderly man whose dark red cardigan had a book poking from one pocket.

Curiosity brimming, Koji asked, "What is the truth about endings?"

Jedrick's answer was like a promise. "They often lead to beginnings."

*In the quiet avenues of the ordinary,
on days like any other,
angels tread back alleys and
front porches, all unseen.
But when it serves God's purposes,
He will open blind eyes—
for a moment, for a miracle.
A foretaste of forever
that begins with a word. When an
angel tells you his name.*

EPILOGUE
THE GIRL IN THE ORCHARD

Koji sat on a window ledge high up in Shimron's tower. The view was spectacular, but he didn't spare it a glance. Black hair fell forward against his cheeks as he bent over a practice page, shaping long rows of letters. The final flourishes were giving him trouble. *Will I always be clumsy? Why can I not achieve Prosper's elegance?*

His pen jerked to a stop, and a blot spread under its tip. Closing his eyes, Koji swallowed past the sudden tightness in his throat. He often thought of questions he wished he could ask Prosper, but that was impossible. All that remained was the memory of Prosper's final words to him. *I wonder.*

Shimron's tower was an archive like no other, and Koji already loved the other members of Jedrick's Flight. But he missed running from lesson to lesson with his middling mentors. And the soft hum of Cherith's bees. And the lessons in Weavers' lore that Weft shared. And Ofir's friendly teasing. *But I have Shimron. And evensong brings the Grafts into the glade for a short time.*

Still, there was a hollow in Koji's heart. And it frightened him a little. *I know I am not alone, so why am I lonely?* Perhaps the sorrow that bound them also set him apart. *My Flightmates are sad, and I am sad. But our reasons are different.*

"Koji?"

His eyes flew open, and he shied away from the warrior who loomed large.

"Peace, little one." Taweel immediately dropped to one knee and held up his hands. He gruffly said, "Forgive me. Do I frighten you?"

Tipping his head to one side, Koji considered the angel. *Guardian. Pierced. Mentor.* With his shaggy black hair, crisscrossing scars, and heavy brows, Taweel had a fearsome appearance. But his ability to intimidate was mostly destroyed by the tiny angel who clung to his earring.

Omri waved, and Koji solemnly waved back.

"I am not afraid." The boy's gaze drifted to the wide rows of stitching and immediately widened. "Why do you bear so many names?"

"I have a Weaver friend. They are his gift to me." Gently tapping the bronze threadwork, Taweel explained, "God entrusted me with the training of newfoundling hadarim in one of heaven's encampments."

"There have been many," Koji murmured, scanning the record.

"Yes." Taweel frowned slightly. "You can read a Weaver's rows?"

"Indeed. One of my mentors was a Weaver."

Taweel grunted. "Mine, too."

Koji blinked. Hadn't Weft mentioned something about teaching a Guardian? Skimming backward to the earliest lines of thread, which was more clumsily wrought than the rest, he found a familiar name. "Mine, too!"

"Wh–?"

But Koji didn't let him finish. Dropping

book and pen, he flung his arms around the big warrior's neck. "Mine, too," he repeated.

Omri's squeaks sparkled like laughter, and Taweel huffed. "Weft was about your size when my lessons began."

"He is big now." In a small voice, Koji added, "And I was not able to say goodbye."

Taweel swathed the boy in his wings. "Why have you not shared this with your mentor? Shimron treasures you."

Koji's lip trembled. "I should be happy here."

"But …?"

"Shimron is a *good* mentor."

Sympathy softened the Guardian's gaze. "And yet …?"

Tears fell, and Koji confessed, "I am often alone."

Big knuckles brushed his cheek. "The members of your new Flight have been lost in their own sorrow. Forgive us for not noticing."

"Why did *you* see?"

"Perhaps because you are so small … and I am accustomed to tending to young ones." Taweel said, "Did you know that when an angel is reassigned, it is customary to gather for one last song."

"It is?"

"We will welcome your friends into our glade." Taweel's deep voice rumbled pleasantly as he banished Koji's troubled thoughts. "Harken will invite them. Abner will bring them. And Baird will lead us all in song."

"Much song?"

"Through all the night watches."

How could I have ever thought Taweel fearsome? He is gentle, and he is kind. And Omri knew it all along. Koji wiggled his fingers at the little angel, who flitted close enough to coo nonsense into his pointed ear. "Taweel?"

He answered with a soft grunt.

"Were you Sent to comfort me?"

"No. I came on Tamaes's behalf."

Koji hadn't spoken with Taweel's apprentice since his first day, when Jedrick introduced them. "He asked for me?"

"No. But I have hope that you are the answer he needs."

One by one, the Grafts of Jedrick's Flight shed their daytime personas to enter the young forest that was their haven. But Koji hardly noticed. Eyes tight shut, he clung to the newest arrival. Cherith still smelled faintly of pollen and beeswax. *Home.*

"Hey, hey, hey, now," came Ofir's over-loud whisper. "Is that a smile?"

"He's *totally* doing that shy smile thing," Baird answered in hushed tones. "Can I be next in line?"

"You?" asked Ofir. "Hugs should be dead easy for a Flightmate. I wouldn't have thought you'd be lacking in such basic luster!"

Koji peeked through his lashes at the cherub, who was as good at being protective as he was at smiling. *Will my first friend scold a First One?*

Ofir wasn't done. "He shouldn't be skimping along, not after Pr–"

Cherith cut him off. "Our very presence is proof of his Flightmates' consideration where Koji's feelings are concerned."

"Oh, man. Have we been neglecting you, Koji?" Suddenly Baird was close enough to bump noses. "I can't tell what you serious types are thinking!"

Serious types? Is Baird referring to his new apprentice? Koji located the reserved Worshiper. By the looks of things, Darda was sketching his harp.

Baird followed his gaze and called, "Say, Kester! Are you short on affection?"

Kester considered his mentor for several moments, then calmly asked, "Are you making a jest in reference to my height?"

Baird rolled his eyes. "Not without calling attention to mine."

Inclining his head, Kester said, "I am adequately supplied."

Easing out of Cherith's embrace, Koji raised his voice enough to be heard by all. "Me, too. I have no complaints."

A sudden swirl of smoky purple light surrounded the boy, scooping him right of his feet. He gasped as strong hands found purchase under his arms. A moment later, he was safely tucked in the crook of a muscular arm.

"Taweel?"

The warrior only grunted, but reassurance whispered through his wings. He strode across the grass to Tamaes, whose conversation trailed off. Darda glanced up from his sketch book, and Kester stepped back to make room. Suddenly, Koji found himself dangling at arms' length. He hung limp, staring wide-eyed into the scarred face of Taweel's apprentice.

Tamaes moved in slow motion, but he obeyed his mentor's implied demand, and the transfer was made. Koji wondered at this strange way of doing things. A peek in Tamaes's direction proved that the bafflement was mutual.

Taweel gruffly said, "See to him."

As he walked away, Tamaes and Koji exchanged another long look.

Kester considered them each in turn, then asked, "To whom was Taweel speaking?"

"Me," they said in unison.

"Tamaes is at the door." Shimron came to sit on the stair where Koji had taken refuge. "He brings an invitation."

"Indeed."

"He mentioned chickens."

Koji's brows drew together. "I have never spoken to him of chickens."

"Nevertheless, he seems to think they will serve as an inducement." Shimron asked, "Why are you reluctant to go out into the created world?"

"Because you do not want me to go."

The ancient angel winced. "Is it so obvious?"

"Fear not." Koji faced his mentor and earnestly promised, "I will stay."

Shimron sighed. "If my fear is what binds you here, then teach me trust by leaving."

"You want me to go because you want me to stay?"

The old angel laughed and took one of Koji's hands. While inspecting the boy's ink-stained fingers, he explained, "I have walked this world often enough to know its dangers. And to know that God is wise. Losing Ephron has shaken me deeply, but I will remain Faithful, just as He is faithful."

Koji turned that over in his mind, and his heart skipped a beat. *This is permission.* Gripping his mentor's hand, Koji said, "If my return will restore your courage, then I will gladly go."

Shimron released him, saying, "Tamaes is waiting."

Koji popped up, padded down the stairs and out the door, straight into Tamaes's watch-care for the afternoon.

In the days that followed, Koji ran between Shimron and Tamaes with increasing frequency. "I am here!" he exclaimed breathlessly.

Tamaes dropped from the barn roof and gave the orchard a searching look. "You should have waited for one of us to escort you!"

"I apologize." Koji ducked his head. "But Omri was with me."

The little angel peeked out from under his hair and hummed happily.

"So I see." Tamaes relaxed into a smile. "Would you like to visit the hens again today?

Or the hayloft?"

Koji shook his head. "The orchard, please. I wish to climb trees like the boys of this family do."

"Have you been watching Zeke?" The Guardian's smile stretched the scar that ran down one side of his face. "His example is hardly one you should follow."

Am I imitating humanity? Koji pondered that for a while, then said, "I liked to climb into trees even before I saw Zeke and his kinfolk. I also enjoy flying. Boys cannot fly."

"Neither can you," Tamaes pointed out.

He is teasing. Having Taweel and Tamaes for Flightmates was almost like having two extra mentors. They liked lessons, questions, and games. *This is a game of hints.* At ease in his Flightmate's arms, Koji gravely inquired, "Am I too great a burden?"

"Never."

With powerful wingbeats, Tamaes carried him swiftly skyward. Koji folded his hands protectively around Omri, but the yahavim was clearly used to the rush. The boy mimicked the little angel's pose, tilting his face into the wind as they climbed to where Taweel flew in lazy circles.

Tamaes asked, "Were you watching over him?"

"More or less," his mentor admitted.

Koji loved flying high over the orchard. *I have no wings, yet my friend carries me on high.* He sobered as the Guardians turned away from the battle lines. *The war is close, yet my friend keeps me closer.*

This was the only thing Koji could do for Tamaes, whose pain over Ephron's disappearance ran deep. *My trust is his comfort. My safety is his reassurance. If only I could do more. Be more.* He frowned thoughtfully. *But what more can I do?*

"There he is! Told you finding him would be dead easy!" Familiar yellow wings cut across Tamaes's path, then swung back around. Ofir called, "Mind if we join you?"

Darda waved his sketchbook. "I was in the mood to paint apples."

Koji leaned forward and waved back. "This is a good place for apples!"

"Too right!" Ofir looked between Koji's

escorts and asked, "Could we borrow our buddy for a bit?"

Tamaes's gaze shifted to Koji and his brows lifted. "Would that please you, Observer?"

"Very much."

While Darda settled in the long grasses beneath a knobbly tree hung with unripe fruit, Koji's attention strayed to a long row of much taller trees. *They are as different from the others as cherubim and adahim, yet they both bear apples. How do humans reach the fruit?* He picked his way down the line, looking for one with low enough branches, but no matter how he stretched, he couldn't find a way up. "Ofir, could you assist me?"

The cherub strolled over. "Need a boost?"

Koji nodded. "I wish to see what these trees see."

"No surprise, given how much you like high places." Ofir bent and nested his fingers together. "Observers and towers go together like wings and sky!"

A light toss and a short scramble found Koji on a limb that was wide enough to be comfortable. He settled with his back to the trunk and pulled one knee to his chest, letting his other leg swing free. *Are adahim made for high places? Is that why we make our homes in towers?* But if that was true, why were Observers so often Sent into the created world for a closer look? *Without this seat, I could not see beyond the first row of apple trees. And without walking amidst the trees, Darda could not see the apples hidden amidst their leaves.*

Ofir interrupted Koji's rambling thoughts. "Your Flightmate is back. And not alone."

Koji's sensitive ears caught the sound of a girl's voice, coming from further along the dusty tracks that disappeared in the direction of a barn. "The daughter of this house is Tamaes's charge. Her name is under his hand."

"Gotcha." Ofir backed away, hands upraised. "Sit tight while I chase down Darda. He's wandered farther than I like."

Koji nodded wisely, for Darda often lost track of time and place.

As the cherub vanished between the trees, a

familiar blaze of bittersweet and amber whirled past. Tamaes flew with sword in hand, but not swiftly, as toward a threat. The Guardian wheeled in widening circles just over the treetops. Reassuringly close. *I am not alone.*

'You have never been alone.'

Awe trembled through Koji's soul, swiftly turning to anticipation. Only he couldn't imagine why.

But all God said was, *'Open your eyes.'*

My eyes? Koji blinked several times, growing more flustered by the moment. People usually praised his ability to see what others missed. Yet his Maker's voice held a note of gentle teasing, as if he was missing something obvious.

Suddenly, the girl's voice sharpened. "Doesn't it feel like someone's watching?"

Koji's attention swung her way. She scanned the orchard much as he had done, then resumed a rambling monologue that seemed to be directed at her feline companion. Which made little sense. *Was this girl not a believer? Why would she pray to a cat?*

"I think it's *sad* that getting the mail is the most exciting part of my day." Putting one foot in front of the other in one of the dusty ruts, she kept right on talking. "If you don't hurry along, we'll miss him!"

The coming of the mail will bring Milo. Would the Messenger have time to visit? Koji had been wanting to ride in his car. Perhaps today would bring a chance.

"Oh!"

The gasp pulled Koji's attention back to the girl, who stood very still. She was staring, and for the first time, it occurred to Koji that God hadn't been speaking to him. And yet wide, blue eyes were carrying out a puzzled inspection.

She stepped closer and asked, "Do you live around here?"

She should not be able to see me. Koji took a shaky breath and asked, "Are you speaking to me?"

The girl answered. "And who *else* would I be talking to?"

She should not be able to see me!

Koji, came the deep voice of Harken, the senior Messenger assigned to Jedrick's Flight. *What's wrong?*

I do not know, the boy replied.

Meanwhile, the girl put on a polite smile. "Hi. I'm Prissie. Prissie Pomeroy." She pointed in the direction she'd come. "I live right over there."

Koji, Harken repeated. *Talk to me. Are you in danger?*

No. But ... she should not be able to see me.

With great patience, Harken said, *Explain, Koji. Who can see you?*

Prissie. The orderly insides of his mind scattered like loose pages, flying in too many directions. *What do I do?*

Shimron's voice came then. *Calm down, Koji, or you may frighten her. While you are not the most fearsome of our kind, you are still foreign. Go gently.*

Harken interjected, *Milo is Sent.*

I am coming! Tamaes exclaimed.

"Do you live around here?" Prissie repeated. "I haven't seen you before. Are you new to the area?"

That much was true, so Koji answered, "I am."

"*That* explains why we haven't met. So what's your name?"

More members of Jedrick's Flight chimed in. Advice. Warnings. Reassurances. One voice drowned out all the others. God asked, *'Do you trust Me?'*

Always.

'Go with her.'

Koji slipped from his perch just as Tamaes arrived, his face suffused with wonder. "Gently," the Guardian urged, reinforcing Shimron's advice. "She sees, but she does not understand."

In obedience to God's command, Koji joined Prissie. *And now what?* He could only go with her if she went somewhere. To calm himself down, Koji began cataloging little details— visible and invisible. The faint blush that might be embarrassment. The measured stare that suggested caution. The arch of fair eyebrows that hinted at impatience.

Into the breathless silence inside his head, Koji reported, *Her hair is the color of honey.*

"I have always thought so," Tamaes said. "But she is waiting for your answer."

An answer? What was the question? Koji searched his scattered thoughts.

Oh, of course. The giving of a name was how beginnings were made. And an exchange of names could forge new bonds. So while he gave his own to her, he wrote hers upon his heart.

"I am called Koji."

About the Author

Behind the scenes, I'm a cheerful homebody whose many talents include dish-washing, laundry-sorting, and the weaving polysyllabic words into everyday conversation. First to know, last to tell, happy to try, and always true. A plotter and a plodder, a dabbler and a devotee. Weaknesses include bright colors, crazy socks, and alliteration. More to the point, I spend my days planning studies, plotting stories, and putting my nose to the proverbial grindstone … because as much as I loves writing, it's work. Finding the perfect word, turning a phrase so it sparkles, giving a plot just a bit of a twist—they're worth every iota of effort. I'm delighted to have discovered what I want to do when I grow up!

Christa also publishes family-friendly fantasy under her maiden name. If you like magical master sculptors, shape-shifting brothers, stowaways with secrets, and mythical creatures, let your curiosity lead you to CJMilbrandt.com.

Threshold Series art, outtakes, and postcards await you on Christa's website. Be sture to drop in for milestone parties, character Q&A sessions, and news about upcoming and ongoing stories.

ChristaKinde.com

Facebook /ChristaKinde

Pinterest /christakinde

Twitter @ChristaKinde

ALSO BY
ᴇHRISTA KINDE

THRESHOLD SERIES

The Blue Door (Book 1)
The Hidden Deep (Book 2)
The Broken Window (Book 3)
The Garden Gate (Book 4)

THRESHOLD COMPANION STORIES

Angels All Around
Angels in Harmony
Angels on Guard
Angel on High
Angel Unaware
Rough and Tumble
Tried and True
Sage and Song

POMEROY FAMILY LEGACY COLLECTION

Pursuing Prissie
Sweets for the Sweet

Angels: A 90-Day Devotional
about God's Messengers

Adventure Begins at the Door

Prissie never expected to stumble into an adventure on her way to the mailbox. Invisible doors, angels in disguise, kidnapped comrades, demonic minions, divine messengers, sword fights, winged rescuers, shared dreams, and apple pie. The Threshold Series by Christa Kinde is appropriate for readers aged eleven and up. Complete in four volumes from Zonderkidz.

Three Free Short Stories

Angels All Around – A divine Messenger becomes one little girl's prince, and a fledgling Guardian becomes their knight.

Angels in Harmony – Angels have always served in pairs, but Baird is sure there must be some mistake when Kester shows up on his doorstep.

Angels on Guard – Tamaes only understood *part* of what it meant to watch over one precious life. The rest he learned on the day he almost lost her.

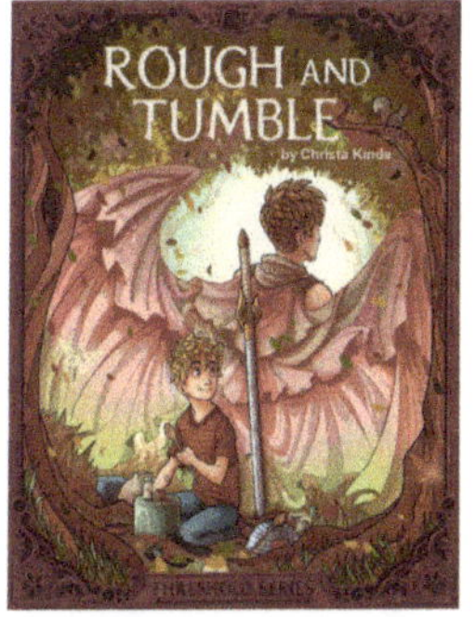

ROUGH AND TUMBLE
by Christa Kinde
THRESHOLD SERIES

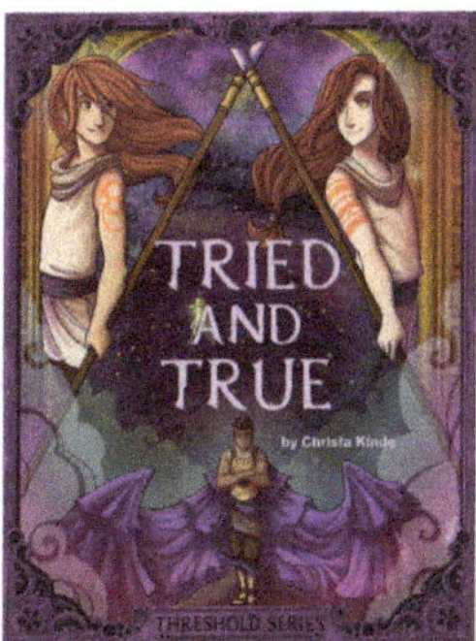

TRIED AND TRUE
by Christa Kinde
THRESHOLD SERIES

ANGELS IN HARMONY
by Christa Kinde
Illustrations by
Anna Earley
THRESHOLD SERIES

ANGELS ON GUARD
by Christa Kinde
Illustrations by
Anna Earley
THRESHOLD SERIES

SAGE AND SONG
by Christa Kinde
THRESHOLD SERIES

ANGEL UNAWARE
by Christa Kinde
THRESHOLD SERIES

FAMILY FRIENDLY FANTASY

Christa writes family-friendly fantasy under her maiden name, C. J. Milbrandt.

Galleries of Stone. Of all the world's treasures, none are more valuable than stone from the Twelve. Children on all four continents are tested for affinity, for the mountains hold magic. But in the foothills of the Gray Mountain, no one remembers stone lore. The majestic Statuary is forgotten, as are the wonders that fill its galleries. Only rumors remain, and those are used to frighten children. For it's said that a monster lives in the heights.

Freydolf serves as the Gray Mountain's Keeper. Exiled. Feared. Unwelcome. But necessity drives him into a Flox village to hire a boy to fetch water and tend fires. Tupper Meadowsweet isn't the cleverest child, but he's brave enough to follow his new master up top. In the Statuary, Tupper finds hints of faraway lands, diverse races, long histories, unique customs, and danger.

Byways Books. Three brothers with a magical inheritance take sibling rivalry to new lengths as they race each other across their homeland. [A multi-book series for kids who are ready for chapter books.]

Byways
2
Aboard the Train
A EWAN JOHNS ADVENTURE

Byways
3
Over the Bridge
A ZANE JOHNS ADVENTURE

Byways
4
Up the Mountain
A GANIX JOHNS ADVENTURE

Byways
5
Inside the Tree
A EWAN JOHNS ADVENTURE

Byways
6
Into the Hills
A ZANE JOHNS ADVENTURE

Byways
7
Across the Line
A GANIX JOHNS ADVENTURE

Byways
8
Down the Stairs
A EWAN JOHNS ADVENTURE

Byways
9
Through the Notches
A ZANE JOHNS ADVENTURE

Byways
10
Back on Track
A GANIX JOHNS ADVENTURE

www.ingramcontent.com/pod-product-compliance
Lightning Source LLC
Chambersburg PA
CBHW042032120726
47911CB00026B/680